Many moons ago, before the arrival of man, the elves and dragons ruled a secret kingdom, hidden from the world outside.

Full epic fairy tale adventure available on audio book, ebook and paperback

Gheldathaw the dragon aided that first ship that arrived carrying people from distant shores.
With the arrival of man, comes change, and seldom is it for the greater good.

Full epic fairy tale adventure available on audio book, ebook and paperback

Take Flight_Colour Palette

1)Black 2)DarkSlateGray 3)DarkSlateGray 4)Brown 5)DarkOliveGreen 6)SeaGreen 7)OliveDrab 8)DimGray 9)IndianRed 10)MediumSeaGreen 11)YellowGreen 12)RosyBrown 13)DarkKhaki 14)DarkSeaGreen 15)DarkGray 16)PaleGoldenRod

As man made these lands their home, it wasn't long before they came into conflict with the natives, particularly the dragons.

As the elves said: a hunting ground shared, is a hunting ground halved.

However, our story begins much earlier, at a time when a vast forest stretched seamlessly from coast to shore. Fact was, that a squirrel could travel the whole length without needing to ever leave the branches of the trees.

Full epic fairy tale adventure available on audio book, ebook and paperback

Back then, the mighty oak trees ruled these lands. Queen Adelaide was once such tree. Slowly her life, her rein, was coming to an end. Soon it would be time to pass on her crown.

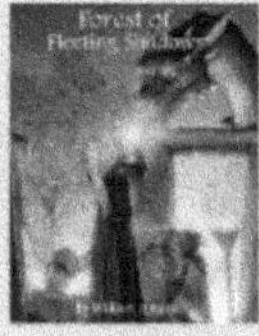

Full epic fairy tale adventure available on audio book, ebook and paperback

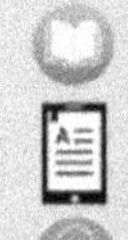

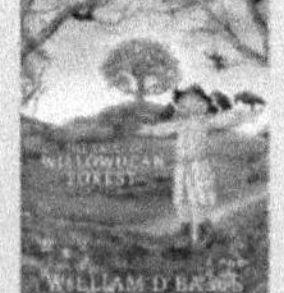

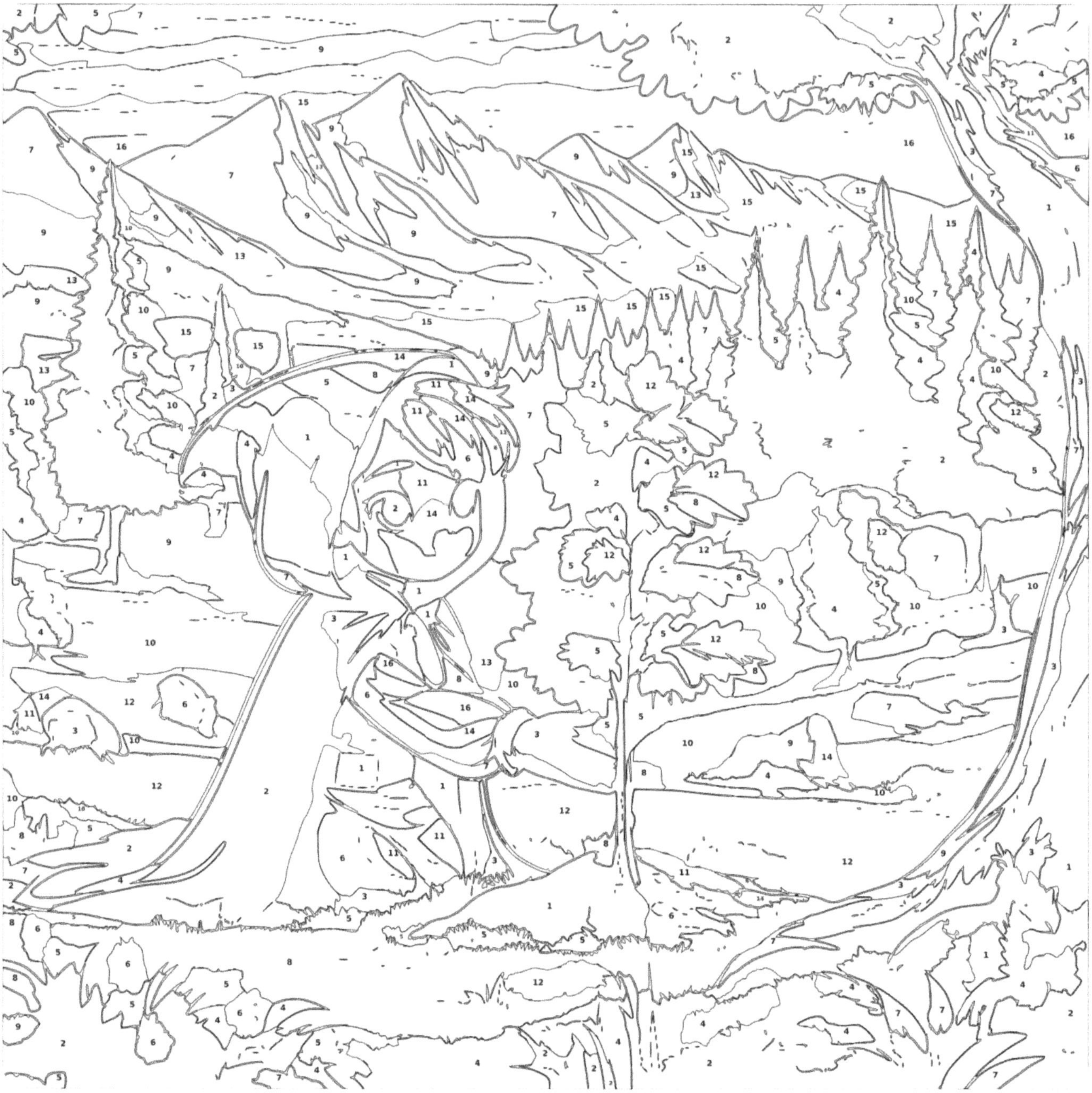

Nurturing_Colour Palette

1)DarkSlateGray 2)DarkSlateGray 3)DarkOliveGreen 4)DarkSlateGray 5)DarkOliveGreen 6)Sienna 7)DimGray 8)OliveDrab 9)SlateGray 10)Gray 11)Peru 12)DarkKhaki 13)DarkSeaGreen 14)Tan 15)LightSteelBlue 16)PaleGoldenRod

Being that royal oak trees seldom bear fruit; a young gardener lends her hand, to ensure a rare and precious acorn has the best chance to germinate.

Donsey, a simple scarecrow, was made long ago by farmer Peach, to protect his crops from those pesky pigeons and crows.

Full epic fairy tale adventure available on audio book, ebook and paperback

George the Scarecrow_Colour Pelette
1)Black 2)Black 3)DarkSlateGray 4)DarkSlateGray 5)SaddleBrown 6)SaddleBrown 7)DimGray 8)DimGray
9)Sienna 10)Gray 11)DarkSeaGreen 12)DarkKhaki 13)BurlyWood 14)LightGray 15)PaleGoldenRod 16)Snow

When farmer Peach grew too old to tend his crops, Donsey found himself abandoned in the overgrown meadow, close to the great Willowdean Forest.

Full epic fairy tale adventure available on audio book, ebook and paperback

Back in the Meadow_Colour Palette
1)DarkSlateGray 2)DarkOliveGreen 3)DarkSlateGray 4)OliveDrab 5)SaddleBrown 6)DimGray 7)Sienna 8)DarkGoldenRod 9)Gray 10)YellowGreen 11)DarkKhaki 12)CadetBlue 13)SkyBlue 14)Silver 15)Khaki 16)PaleTurquoise

Luckily, Donsey was found by two children, Billy & Sarah. They took our scarecrow to a dusty old barn to make him good again. Once they had finished they gave him a new name. They called him George.

A precious dragling begins its life. Despite the expected longevity of a dragon, they rarely produce offspring.

Full epic fairy tale adventure available on audio book, ebook and paperback

First Flight_Colour Palette
1)DarkSlateGray 2)SaddleBrown 3)DarkOliveGreen 4)DarkSlateGray 5)SaddleBrown 6)Teal 7)DimGray
8)Chocolate 9)DarkCyan 10)DarkGoldenRod 11)Gray 12)CadetBlue 13)Peru 14)MediumAquaMarine 15)Tan
16)LightGray

It was a celebration indeed, when Salgander, partner to Gheldathaw, hatched not one, but two draglings that spring.

Full epic fairy tale adventure available on audio book, ebook and paperback

Gheldathaw the Dragon_Colour Pelette
1)DarkSlateGray 2)DarkOliveGreen 3)Teal 4)Sienna 5)SeaGreen 6)SteelBlue 7)DimGray 8)YellowGreen
9)CadetBlue 10)LightSeaGreen 11)Tomato 12)RosyBrown 13)SkyBlue 14)Tan 15)PowderBlue 16)Beige

Dragling's are vulnerable creatures. A warm, safe nursery is vital for their early years.

Full epic fairy tale adventure available on audio book, ebook and paperback

It was in part thanks to George the scarecrow, that Thoden & Ellenor, finally stood together upon that lofty mound. Thereafter, Queen Adelaide renounced her crown to her son. So it was, that Thoden & Ellenore became king and queen of Willowdean Forest.

Full epic fairy tale adventure available on audio book, ebook and paperback

Royal Trees_Colour Palette

1)DarkSlateGray 2)SaddleBrown 3)DarkOliveGreen 4)Sienna 5)SeaGreen 6)OliveDrab 7)DimGray 8)Chocolate
9)SlateGray 10)Peru 11)YellowGreen 12)GoldenRod 13)DarkSeaGreen 14)RosyBrown 15)Khaki 16)Gainsboro

Thanks to a secret rescue party, George the scarecrow was freed from that dusty old barn, up on the hill.

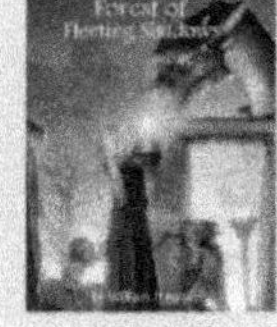

Full epic fairy tale adventure available on audio book, ebook and paperback

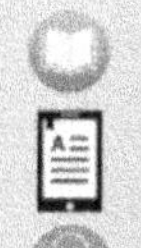

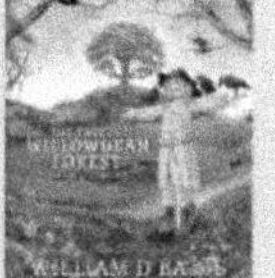

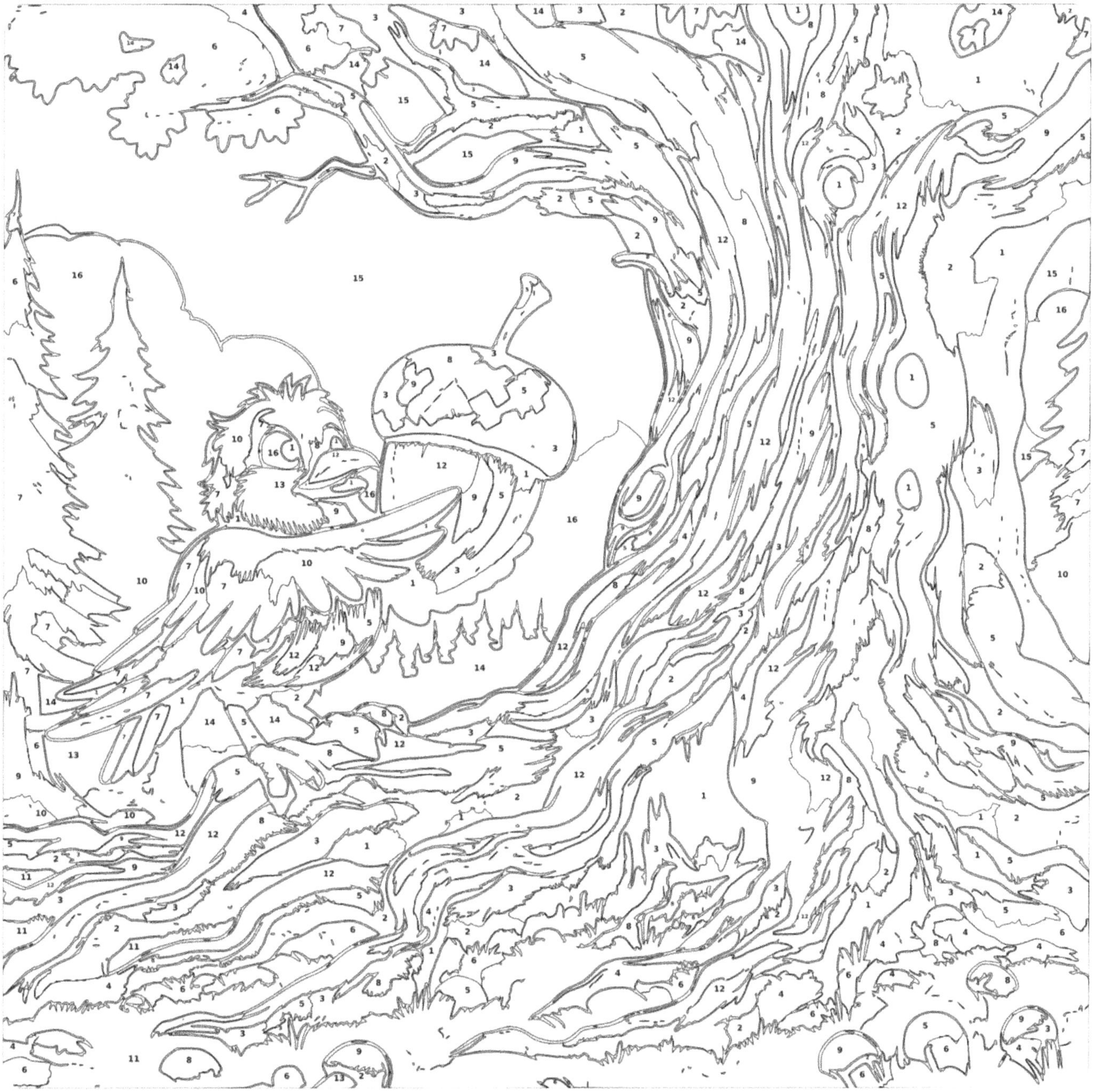

From tiny acorns_Colour Palette
1)Black 2)Black 3)DarkSlateGray 4)SaddleBrown 5)SaddleBrown 6)DarkOliveGreen 7)DimGray 8)Sienna 9)Sienna 10)Gray 11)Peru 12)Peru 13)Tan 14)DarkGray 15)PaleTurquoise 16)WhiteSmoke

And so he returned to the meadow to stand side by side with his King and Queen.

Far away from others, deep within the forest, live a tribe of goblins. Their favourite ritual is to ride a wild boar through the forest.

Many learnt that a hog can be a fearsome swine once angered.

Full epic fairy tale adventure available on audio book, ebook and paperback

Hog Goblin_Colour_Palette
1)Black 2)Black 3)SaddleBrown 4)DarkOliveGreen 5)Brown 6)DarkOliveGreen 7)Sienna 8)Gray 9)IndianRed
10)DarkKhaki 11)RosyBrown 12)RosyBrown 13)DarkKhaki 14)BurlyWood 15)Silver 16)LightGoldenRodYellow

One such ride led the goblins right to the edge of the forest. They saw for the first time the twinkle of lights from a village of men.

Full epic fairy tale adventure available on audio book, ebook and paperback

Goblins_Colour Palette
1)Black 2)DarkSlateGray 3)DarkSlateGray 4)DarkOliveGreen 5)DarkOliveGreen 6)DimGray 7)Sienna
8)SlateGray 9)CadetBlue 10)Peru 11)DarkSeaGreen 12)MediumAquaMarine 13)BurlyWood 14)PaleGreen
15)Khaki 16)Wheat

Three young goblins, inquisitive, but devilish by nature. Was it this that led them to carry out the unspeakable deed upon a family from the village.

Sapphire the young witch maiden was strolling through the forest when she happened across a despairing wolf pup.

Full epic fairy tale adventure available on audio book, ebook and paperback

Wolf Pup_Colour Palette
1)Black 2)SaddleBrown 3)DarkOliveGreen 4)SaddleBrown 5)DarkSlateGray 6)DarkSlateBlue 7)OliveDrab 8)Sienna 9)SlateGray 10)Gray 11)Peru 12)CadetBlue 13)SandyBrown 14)BurlyWood 15)LightSteelBlue 16)Gainsboro

She rescued the puppy, took him back to her home in the forest, adopted him, loved him. Sapphire named her wolf, Faolan.

Full epic fairy tale adventure available on audio book, ebook and paperback

Faolan the Wolf_Colour Palette
1)Black 2)DarkSlateGray 3)DarkSlateGray 4)DarkSlateGray 5)DarkOliveGreen 6)DimGray 7)Sienna 8)SlateGray
9)DimGray 10)CadetBlue 11)DarkKhaki 12)LightSteelBlue 13)BurlyWood 14)Silver 15)PaleTurquoise 16)Beige

As Faolan grew, so he became more and more mindful to the call of the wild.

Sapphire learns the gossip of the forest as the stag conveys his news.

Full epic fairy tale adventure available on audio book, ebook and paperback

Friends_Colour Palette
1)DarkOliveGreen 2)SaddleBrown 3)DarkOliveGreen 4)DimGray 5)MediumSeaGreen 6)Gray 7)YellowGreen
8)Gray 9)Peru 10)RosyBrown 11)CadetBlue 12)DarkGray 13)BurlyWood 14)Silver 15)LightBlue 16)Gainsboro

Fact is, that the witch loved her life, and everything that nature's great basket had to offer. That was, until jealousy spurned by another, tricked her down a dark and perilous path.

Full epic fairy tale adventure available on audio book, ebook and paperback

Friends_Colour Palette
1)DarkSlateGray 2)DarkSlateGray 3)DarkOliveGreen 4)DimGray 5)DimGray 6)DimGray 7)DimGray 8)SlateGray 9)Gray 10)LightSlateGray 11)RosyBrown 12)DarkGray 13)Silver 14)Silver 15)AntiqueWhite 16)Beige

The wild hart conveys a message of love, between a man mortal and a young witch maiden.

Full epic fairy tale adventure available on audio book, ebook and paperback

The wrath of Gheldathaw would be felt by many, as he searches to find the men who perpetrated that crime against his family.

Full epic fairy tale adventure available on audio book, ebook and paperback

Revenge_Colour Palette
1)Black 2)DarkSlateGray 3)SaddleBrown 4)DarkOliveGreen 5)Sienna 6)DimGray 7)SteelBlue 8)Gray 9)Peru
10)CadetBlue 11)LightSlateGray 12)DarkKhaki 13)SkyBlue 14)Khaki 15)PaleTurquoise 16)Snow

Such a crime leads to dire consequences, although in this event, things are not always black and white.

Full epic fairy tale adventure available on audio book, ebook and paperback

Village ablaze_Colour Palette
1)DarkSlateGray 2)DarkOliveGreen 3)SaddleBrown 4)DarkOliveGreen 5)DimGray 6)Sienna 7)DimGray
8)Chocolate 9)Peru 10)CadetBlue 11)Peru 12)DarkSeaGreen 13)SandyBrown 14)DarkSeaGreen 15)Khaki
16)BlanchedAlmond

Not just the guilty suffer from a dragon's reprisal.

Full epic fairy tale adventure available on audio book, ebook and paperback

The menacing meeting upon the Kassum Bridge was not as it appeared,

Full epic fairy tale adventure available on audio book, ebook and paperback

Bridge to cross_Colour Palette
1)DarkSlateGray 2)DarkSlateGray 3)DarkSlateGray 4)DimGray 5)DimGray 6)DimGray 7)DimGray 8)SlateGray 9)Gray 10)DarkSeaGreen 11)RosyBrown 12)DarkGray 13)DarkGray 14)Tan 15)PowderBlue 16)Beige

You may go unchallenged, Old Crow, said the troll. But should you return by this bridge, then I shall learn your name and your business, ere you pass.

Full epic fairy tale adventure available on audio book, ebook and paperback

Troll Bridge_Colour Palette
1)DarkSlateGray 2)DarkSlateGray 3)SaddleBrown 4)DarkOliveGreen 5)DarkOliveGreen 6)DarkOliveGreen
7)Sienna 8)Gray 9)Peru 10)Gray 11)DarkKhaki 12)DarkSeaGreen 13)Tan 14)LightSteelBlue 15)PowderBlue
16)HoneyDew

What then, if we do cross this bridge, for not all trolls eat children.

Full epic fairy tale adventure available on audio book, ebook and paperback

Elgarth the old wizard, comes to the call of a tiny dragling.
She should have been safe in her cave, her nursery.

Full epic fairy tale adventure
available on audio book, ebook
and paperback

Moonstone jewel_Colour Palette
1)Black 2)Black 3)DarkSlateGray 4)DarkSlateGray 5)SaddleBrown 6)DimGray 7)Sienna 8)Sienna 9)Gray
10)Gray 11)DarkKhaki 12)DarkKhaki 13)DarkGray 14)BurlyWood 15)Tan 16)PaleGoldenRod

As Elgarth puts two and two together he realises the dragon's malice that will ensue.

Suddenly there came a quaking, a splitting of the earth. Elgarth and the dragling became trapped within the dragon's cave as the only entrance collapsed to darkness.

Full epic fairy tale adventure available on audio book, ebook and paperback

Stone by rock, Elgarth the wizard worked tirelessly, until he had freed the entrance to that cave. When the new day broke, a shaft of morning sun offered rays of hope.

Full epic fairy tale adventure available on audio book, ebook and paperback

When is it ever the right time to say goodbye. For mortals, life slips by all too quickly.

Full epic fairy tale adventure available on audio book, ebook and paperback

farewell_Colour Palette
1)Black 2)DarkSlateGray 3)DarkOliveGreen 4)DarkOliveGreen 5)Sienna 6)DimGray 7)DimGray 8)Gray
9)Gray 10)Gray 11)DarkSalmon 12)DarkKhaki 13)DarkSeaGreen 14)BurlyWood 15)Wheat 16)Beige

When Sapphire stumbled across a hidden trapper's lodge, she discovered the truth about a man's obsession to destroy god's creatures.

Full epic fairy tale adventure available on audio book, ebook and paperback

Best of Friends_Colour Palette
1)Black 2)Black 3)DarkSlateGray 4)DarkOliveGreen 5)DarkSlateGray 6)DimGray 7)DarkOliveGreen 8)DimGray 9)Gray 10)Peru 11)RosyBrown 12)DarkSeaGreen 13)DarkSalmon 14)Silver 15)Tan 16)LightGray

The witch's confrontation with that trapper, invoked the worst of the man's arrogance.

Just when this thug believed he could do just as he wished with Sapphire, nature, along with a spell of magic, repelled his vial advances and reaped havoc upon the blighter.

A Plague of Flies_Colour Palette
1)Black 2)SaddleBrown 3)DarkSlateGray 4)SaddleBrown 5)DarkSlateGray 6)DimGray 7)OliveDrab 8)IndianRed 9)LightSlateGray 10)RosyBrown 11)DarkSalmon 12)SkyBlue 13)DarkGray 14)BurlyWood 15)Wheat 16)LightGray

Sapphire learns the ugly truth to the extent of the animals suffering, caused by one man's greed.

Full epic fairy tale adventure available on audio book, ebook and paperback

Flies_Colour Palette

1)Black 2)Maroon 3)DarkOliveGreen 4)SaddleBrown 5)DarkSlateGray 6)Sienna 7)OliveDrab 8)SeaGreen 9)Peru 10)LightSlateGray 11)DarkKhaki 12)SandyBrown 13)DarkGray 14)BurlyWood 15)PaleGoldenRod 16)PowderBlue

A plague of insects drove this swine to madness. Finally, he threw himself into a stagnant pool of water to ease the stinging.

Eons ago, the elves mined and fashioned the most beautiful and precious jewel. Within the pure carbon facets was secreted magic of elvish craft. Named the Moonstone jewel, it was gifted to the dragons as a mark of friendship and trust.

Full epic fairy tale adventure available on audio book, ebook and paperback

Finding the Jewel_Colour Palette
1)Black 2)DarkSlateGray 3)MidnightBlue 4)DarkSlateGray 5)SaddleBrown 6)Teal 7)DimGray 8)Sienna
9)Peru 10)SteelBlue 11)SteelBlue 12)Gray 13)DarkSeaGreen 14)MediumTurquoise 15)Khaki 16)PaleTurquoise

Gheldathaw the dragon was the chosen keeper and guardian of the Moonstone jewel.

Full epic fairy tale adventure available on audio book, ebook and paperback

Jewel_Colour Palette
1)DarkSlateGray 2)DarkSlateGray 3)DarkSlateGray 4)Teal 5)DimGray 6)DimGray 7)DarkCyan 8)DimGray
9)CadetBlue 10)LightSeaGreen 11)DarkSeaGreen 12)RosyBrown 13)MediumTurquoise 14)Khaki 15)LightBlue
16)Beige

Magic in the wrong hands will lead to disaster...

Seeking to reclaim their precious jewel. the dragons shall leave no stone unturned, until they possess it again.

Full epic fairy tale adventure available on audio book, ebook and paperback

DragonAmbush_Colour Palette
1)Black 2)DarkSlateGray 3)DarkSlateGray 4)DarkOliveGreen 5)DimGray 6)Sienna 7)SeaGreen 8)Gray 9)Peru
10)DarkKhaki 11)CadetBlue 12)RosyBrown 13)Silver 14)BurlyWood 15)PowderBlue 16)Gainsboro

The good folk of Dillington arrive to ferry innocent victims back to their shire.

Full epic fairy tale adventure
available on audio book, ebook
and paperback

Dragon Rage_Colour Palette
1)DarkSlateGray 2)SaddleBrown 3)DarkOliveGreen 4)Sienna 5)DarkCyan 6)OliveDrab 7)DimGray 8)SlateGray
9)IndianRed 10)DarkSeaGreen 11)DarkKhaki 12)MediumTurquoise 13)Tan 14)BurlyWood 15)LightBlue
16)Gainsboro

Not everyone made it back to the village of Dillington. Some lost a lot more than just their belongings.

Full epic fairy tale adventure available on audio book, ebook and paperback

The secret elven kingdom of Muscaria is where legends are born. Throughout the kingdoms they are recited to the little ones, by the fire, and by the eerie light of a full moon.

Full epic fairy tale adventure available on audio book, ebook and paperback

Hidden kingdom_Colour Palette

1)DarkSlateGray 2)DarkOliveGreen 3)DarkSlateGray 4)DimGray 5)Sienna 6)Sienna 7)Peru 8)Gray
9)RosyBrown 10)Peru 11)RosyBrown 12)SandyBrown 13)BurlyWood 14)Silver 15)PaleGoldenRod 16)OldLace

Saffron has a darker side, hidden from all by her charm, her beauty.

Full epic fairy tale adventure available on audio book, ebook and paperback

Fairy dance_Colour Palette
1)Maroon 2)DarkSlateGray 3)SaddleBrown 4)DimGray 5)Olive 6)Sienna 7)Gray 8)Peru 9)Peru 10)Peru
11)RosyBrown 12)SandyBrown 13)LightCoral 14)BurlyWood 15)Khaki 16)Bisque

Only at special occasions will fairies dance during the heat of the summer sun.

From an early age she had the gift to bring them to life. As well, she could easily take it away.

Full epic fairy tale adventure available on audio book, ebook and paperback

Bought to life_Colour Palette
1)Black 2)DarkSlateGray 3)DarkSlateGray 4)DarkOliveGreen 5)DarkOliveGreen 6)DimGray 7)SeaGreen
8)DimGray 9)Gray 10)SlateGray 11)DarkKhaki 12)DarkSeaGreen 13)DarkGray 14)BurlyWood 15)Silver
16)Wheat

Dancing and twisting like spirits of the night, Dilly and Donsey, relished their new lives.

Full epic fairy tale adventure available on audio book, ebook and paperback

Not simply a scarecrow_Colour Palette

1)Black 2)DarkSlateGray 3)DarkSlateGray 4)DarkOliveGreen 5)DarkSlateGray 6)DarkSlateGray
7)DarkOliveGreen 8)DimGray 9)Peru 10)Gray 11)CadetBlue 12)DarkKhaki 13)DarkSeaGreen 14)Tan
15)BurlyWood 16)LightGray

The sad tale of what became of Dilly, would not be known until Donsey found his conscience.

Full epic fairy tale adventure available on audio book, ebook and paperback

Do Elves become fairies_Colour Free Style

This scene has little to do with the story thus far. But what is a fairy tale without fairies.
Please share your colouring thoughts and look out for part 2.